BOOK CLUB IN A BOX

Bookclub-in-a-Box presents the discussion companion for Mark Haddon's novel

the curious incident of the dog in the night-time

Published by Anchor Canada, 2004, a division of Random House of Canada Limited.   ISBN: 0-385-65980-6

Quotations used in this guide have been taken from the text of the paperback edition of **the curious incident of the dog in the night-time**. All information taken from other sources is acknowledged.

This discussion companion for **the curious incident of the dog in the night-time** has been prepared and written by Marilyn Herbert, originator of Bookclub-in-a-Box. Marilyn Herbert. B.Ed., is a teacher, librarian, speaker and writer. Bookclub-in-a-Box is a unique guide to current fiction and classic literature intended for book club discussions, educational study seminars, and personal pleasure. For more information about the Bookclub-in-a-Box team, visit our website.

Bookclub-in-a-Box discussion companion for the curious incident of the dog in the night-time

ISBN 10: 1-897082-11-8
ISBN 13: 9781897082119

This guide reflects the perspective of the Bookclub-in-a-Box team and is the sole property of Bookclub-in-a-Box.

CONTACT INFORMATION: SEE BACK COVER.

BOOKCLUB-IN-A-BOX

Mark Haddon's the curious incident of the dog in the nighttime

BOOKCLUB-IN-A-BOX

Readers and Leaders Guide

Each Bookclub-in-a-Box guide is clearly and effectively organized to give you information and ideas for a lively discussion, as well as to present the major highlights of the novel. The format, with a Table of Contents, allows you to pick and choose the specific points you wish to talk about. It does not have to be used in any prescribed order. In fact, it is meant to support, not determine, your discussion.

You Choose What to Use.

You may find that some information is repeated in more than one section and may be cross-referenced so as to provide insight on the same idea from different angles.

The guide is formatted to give you extra space to make your own notes.

How to Begin

Relax and look forward to enjoying your bookclub.

With Bookclub-in-a-Box as your behind the scenes support, there is little for you to do in the way of preparation.

Some readers like to review the guide after reading the novel; some before. Either way, the guide is all you will need as a companion for your discussion. You may find that the guide's interpretation, information, and background have sparked other ideas not included.

Having read the novel and armed with Bookclub-in-a-Box, you will be well prepared to lead or guide or listen to the discussion at hand.

Lastly, if you need some more 'hands-on' support, feel free to contact us. (See Contact Information)

What to Look For

Each Bookclub-in-a-Box guide is divided into easy-to-use sections, which include points on characters, themes, writing style and structure, literary or historical background, author information, and other pertinent features unique to the novel being discussed. These may vary slightly from guide to guide.

INTERPRETATION OF EACH NOVEL REFLECTS THE PERSPECTIVE OF THE BOOKCLUB-IN-A-BOX TEAM.

Do We Need to Agree?

THE ANSWER TO THIS QUESTION IS NO.

If we have sparked a discussion or a debate on certain points, then we are happy. We invite you to share your group's alternative findings and experiences with us. You can respond on-line at our website or contact us through our Contact Information. We would love to hear from you.

Discussion Starters

There are as many ways to begin a bookclub discussion as there are members in your group. If you are an experienced group, you will already have your favorite ways to begin. If you are a newly formed group or a group looking for new ideas, here are some suggestions.

Ask for people's impressions of the novel. (This will give you some idea about which parts of the unit to focus on.)

- Identify a favorite or major character.

- Identify a favorite or major idea.

- Begin with a powerful or pertinent quote. (not necessarily from the novel)

- Discuss the historical information of the novel. (not applicable to all novels)

- If this author is familiar to the group, discuss the range of his/her work and where this novel stands in that range.

- Use the discussion topics and questions in the Bookclub-in-a-Box guide.

If you have further suggestions for discussion starters, be sure to share them with us and we will share them with others.

Above All, Enjoy Yourselves

INTRODUCTION

Suggested Beginnings

Novel Quickline

Key to the Novel

Author Information

INTRODUCTION

Suggested Beginnings

Mark Haddon's book deals with the neurological disorder, Asperger's Syndrome, that has to date not been explored in a fictional framework. Consider your group's reactions to the novel and begin with any or all of the following questions.

1. *"Reading is a conversation. All books talk. But a good book listens as well."* (Guardian interview with author)

What does Mark Haddon mean by this? Discuss his quote in connection to this novel.

2. Haddon has accomplished the literary feat of entering the mind and spirit of a person with Asperger's Syndrome and conveying it with accuracy and compassion.

What is the role of Christopher as the narrator? Connect and compare his function in this novel to the narrators in other novels.

3. Christopher has so many difficulties that it would be natural for the reader to feel sympathy or pity for him. Yet, there is also a feeling of triumph in Christopher's tale.

Consider your emotional reaction to Christopher in both a literary and personal sense.

4. Christopher's mother postponed his math A-level exam, claiming that he would be unable to take it because he was living in London with her. (p.209)

What were her motives? Assess Christopher's mother in terms of her personality and her relationship with Christopher.

5. Christopher has no typical emotional reactions to anyone, including his own parents, yet we see each parent clearly through Christopher's eyes.

Discuss each parent in terms of reader reaction and sympathy (or lack of sympathy). Discuss the relationship of each to Christopher.

More Questions

6. the curious incident of the dog in the nighttime was published as both an adult and teen novel.

Into which genre does the novel fit best – adult or young adult? Does the novel work equally well in both genres? Is the crossover effect successful?

7. Some readers, including Haddon himself, find the curious incident of the dog in the nighttime to be funny. Still others see the presence of "bad language" as inappropriate for children. (see Author, p.12)

Is there humor in this novel? How does the humor fit with Haddon's presentation of a character like Christopher? Would this novel be a negative influence on children?

8. Readers respond to a novel because they are either drawn to the characters or to the plot. Plot-driven books are designed to entertain; character-driven books are designed to explain. Haddon says that he did not feel confident that anyone would want to read about a young boy with a neurological handicap; therefore he wanted to construct an appealing plot.

Where on the literary spectrum would you place Haddon's novel? What is the book's best feature – the character, Christopher, or the plot?

9. Christopher is probably the first character with Asperger's Syndrome to be portrayed in fiction. Consider the format of a novel dealing with autism as compared with a non-fiction book discussing this same condition.

What is the effect on the reader? Which format presents more accurate information about this disorder? Which is more effective in conveying the information? Which do you prefer?

10. Clearly Christopher has Asperger's Syndrome.

Why does Haddon not identify this syndrome?

Novel Quickline

- Christopher John Francis Boone is confronted with a mystery when he finds his neighbor's dog dead of a fatal stab wound inflicted by a set of garden shears. An animal lover, Christopher is determined to solve the mystery and find the murderer.

- However, this is not the only mystery in Christopher's life. His mother disappeared suddenly two years earlier and Christopher had been told that she had died. In the unraveling of the mystery surrounding the dog, Christopher discovers that his mother is still alive. Now Christopher has two mysteries to solve.

- Normally, exploratory situations such as these would be tackled through the methods of investigation and questioning, both of which involve approaching people to discover their observations and hear their answers. Interaction such as this is common for most people, but not for Christopher.

- Because Christopher has Asperger's Syndrome, a form of autism, he does not like approaching people he does not know. This makes investigation difficult, but Christopher does like to solve puzzles. However, his father has made him solemnly promise not to pursue the incident, and so Christopher experiences the full intensity of these conflicting emotions. He must decide whether or not to continue the search on behalf of a dead dog and a missing mother.

- What seems commonplace and attainable for ordinary people is anything but for Christopher. Solving these two mysteries will take every ounce of effort and ingenuity that Christopher has. Mark Haddon has created a first person narrator who bravely faces his personal challenges. Over the course of the story, we are taken into the head and thoughts of an unusual young man. We not only learn about him, but about ourselves as well.

notes

Key to the novel

Counterexample

- When Christopher writes his math A-level exam, he is asked to solve a problem involving right-angled triangles. In the solution to this problem, Christopher must use a counterexample to disprove the converse to a statement about these triangles.

- Behind this thinking is the established, and always correct, Pythagorean theorem for a right-angled triangle. (see Pythagoras, p.60) Christopher's challenge is to use a counterexample (a reversed formula) to show there can be a right-angled triangle whose measurements do not fit the traditional theory.

  STATEMENT:
  A triangle with sides that can be written in the form of $n2 + 1$, $n2 - 1$ and $2n$ (where $n>1$) is right-angled.

  CONVERSE STATEMENT:
  A triangle that is right-angled has sides whose lengths can be written in the form $n2 = 1$, $n2- 1$ and $2n$ (where $n>1$).

  CHALLENGE:
  To prove that the converse to the original statement is incorrect.

- Christopher uses a right-angled triangle (ABC, p.226) to show that it does not have sides that can be written according to the test formula.

- Mark Haddon is a math wizard, and just like Christopher, he likes to solve complex problems. In this novel, Haddon shows off both his exceptional math skills and his exceptional literary skills by creating a character who displays characteristics consistent with the complex and special needs of a person with Asperger's Syndrome. Although the distinctive Asperger's characteristics fit Christopher accurately, Haddon's protagonist is more complex than expected, showing different and insightful sides of himself that exceed the clinical definition.

Christopher, himself, is Haddon's literary counterexample.

Author Information

Personal Information and Career

- Mark Haddon is British, born in Northampton, England in 1962. Following the completion of his undergraduate degree in English, Haddon worked for a while as a volunteer with children and adults who suffered from a variety of physical and mental disabilities. Then he turned to writing.

- Before the publication of **the curious incident of the dog in the nighttime**, Haddon's work did not register on the literary scene at large despite the fact, or because of the fact, that he was primarily a writer of children's books. To date, he has produced and illustrated seventeen books. He entered the children's book market because he felt it might be easier than writing for adults, but he quickly learned that creating a comprehensive and valuable book for children, which may only contain a potential maximum of twelve words, is a very difficult task.

- He believes that writing for children is in many ways more challenging than writing for adults, and he feels a responsibility for moving young readers *"along the spectrum from Where's Spot? to Mrs. Dalloway."*

- Haddon began to feel the desire to write while still a teenager, but he planned to enroll at Oxford as a math student. He made a last-minute, and fateful, decision to switch from the study of math to English Literature.

- Mark Haddon is currently a teacher of creative writing in Oxford, England, where he lives with his family: his wife, also a teacher, and their young son, Alfie. In addition to his literary interests, he plays sports, kayaks, paints, and is a devoted science reader. Haddon is a multi-talented thinker who can do math as easily as he can write a novel. He considers himself lucky in the writing of this book, as he was able to incorporate both his skills and his interests.

- In his forties, Mark Haddon is a new generation of writer: young, enthusiastic, and very friendly. He has a casual and carefree manner, and an earring in one ear, which appears to challenge his identity as a serious writer of literary fiction.

Accomplishments and Awards

- This novel has won considerable recognition and was published simultaneously as adult and teen fiction:

    - Commonwealth Writer's Prize, 2004.

    - Alex Award, 2004, which honors an adult book that captures the attention of teen readers, ages 12-18. (Other Alex winners include **The Kite Runner** and **The Time Traveler's Wife**.) The Alex award is named for Margaret Alexander Edwards,

a Baltimore librarian who specialized in literature for young adults. Her goal was to extend their experiences in an effort to increase and enrich their understanding of themselves and their environment.

- Whitbread Best Book of the Year and a New York Times Notable Book; the Los Angeles Times Book Prize; a Today Show Book Club selection.

- The novel is an international hit and has spread like wildfire throughout the world. The film rights have been purchased by Warner Brothers, Heyday Films, and Brad Pitt and Brad Grey. The screenwriter of the Harry Potter film series, Steve Kloves, is the writer and director of the film, **the curious incident of the dog in the nighttime,** which has been announced and is in production.

- In the fall of 2006, Haddon published and released a new novel called **A Spot of Bother,** one which is defined as adult fiction. Its previous working title, *Blood and Scissors,* leaves no mistake that this will not be a novel about innocence, nor about a rite of passage. In fact it is a domestic comedy and deals with sex, death, and madness. Light reading material ...

Philosophy of Writing

- Haddon is interested in the effect of literary fiction on the reader. One of his goals in writing **the curious incident of the dog in the nighttime** is to give readers the opportunity to open the boundaries of their thoughts and experience in relation to a little known character like Christopher.

- In portraying Christopher, Haddon wants us to observe how we see ourselves in our perfectly normal spheres next to others, whose spheres may be less than perfect. For Haddon, the importance of this exercise is not to try to understand Christopher, but to understand who we are in relation to Christopher. Christopher himself tells us we are not so different from him **(p.43, 44)** and our needs may be just as "special" as his. Haddon's literary treatment of Christopher is respectful and sympathetic.

- Haddon's novel shows that fiction can promote and provoke imagination rather than just provide feelings of escapism.

- Haddon also feels that his novel has humor and hopes that it is provocatively positive. He would like his story to break down any barriers that exist between ourselves and others whom we may not fully understand.

- The seed for his novel came to Haddon through a picture of a dog, dead from a garden fork stab wound. This act was to be the result of a terrible adult action, although the image, according to Haddon, felt cartoon-like. When he considered this image, he thought of it as comical, but only if it were described in a flat voice devoid of emotion. Upon further reflection, he realized that he liked the tone of the voice in his head and he developed the owner of the voice into the character, Christopher.

- Interestingly, Haddon claims Jane Austen as a model for his work because she wrote affectionately and sympathetically about the ordinary women of her times, women whose lives were bound by the strict rules of their society. She fashioned her books into the kinds of romantic stories that would give her readers pleasure.

- Haddon copies this aspect of Austen by taking Christopher, a protagonist with a very constrained existence, and places him into a murder mystery, which is exactly the kind of book Christopher himself likes. In doing so, Haddon encourages the reader to imagine Christopher beyond the limitations that he shows. In this way, he expands Christopher's life and nature. Although Christopher himself is uncomfortable with the use of imagination, Haddon knows that the reader is not.

- The novel's title originates with Sir Conan Doyle's book **Silver Blaze** in which Sherlock Holmes investigates a middle-of-the-night theft of a very expensive racehorse. When asked to what the inspector's attention should be drawn, Holmes answers: *"To the curious incident of the dog in the night-time ... The dog did nothing in the nighttime ... that was the curious incident."*

notes

CHARACTERIZATION

Christopher

Christopher's Parents

Mr. and Mrs. Shears

Mrs. Alexander

Siobhan

CHARACTERIZATION   *... a note about*

- The world of an autistic child is necessarily small and contained. In keeping with this idea, the number of individuals in this book is also small. Christopher is the primary character as well as the first-person narrator. The other people with whom Christopher interacts are those in his personal sphere of existence. As the story progresses, Christopher reaches outside this sphere and makes contact, sometimes voluntarily, but mostly involuntarily, with others.

- Haddon successfully shows Christopher's daily stress and bewilderment alongside the stress and bewilderment of Christopher's parents and others whom he encounters. Despite his high level of functionality in some areas, Christopher is clearly what society has termed a "special needs" child.

notes

- The characters fall into the following categories: parents, teacher, neighbors, police, and the general public. The novel, like Christopher's path to the train station, moves outward in ever-widening circles from the central incident of the story, the murder of the dog, to his journey to London. By the time Christopher has returned to his home, his abilities and understanding have expanded, and so have ours.

The characters are as follows:

- Christopher John Francis Boone
- Mother and father
- Siobhan, Christopher's teacher
- Mrs. Shears, owner of Wellington, the dog
- Mr. Shears, who is in a relationship with Christopher's mother
- Mrs. Alexander, the kindly neighbor who tries to befriend Christopher
- Rhodri, the father's plumbing assistant
- Toby the rat, Christopher's pet
- The policemen who encounter Christopher in a number of situations.

Christopher John Francis Boone

Christopher most likely has Asperger's Syndrome. **(see Autism, p.58)** He has strong likes and dislikes and is highly sensitive to his surrounding environment. His heightened awareness leads him to continually assess his world and try to make sense of it.

What Christopher can and cannot do:

CAN DO:

- Christopher is a logical rather than a linear thinker, preferring concrete and visual images. He thinks in similes, not metaphors. Christopher believes that all things can eventually be proved through math and science.
- He understands and loves computers, order, timetables, and schedules – all of which fill his need for boundaries. He likes small, well-bounded spaces, but at the same time he likes the concept of outer space, where there are no people.
- Christopher is very observant and has a photographic memory, which he thinks of as a searchable computer file. He has great powers of concentration and can focus exclusively on a single item or thought.
- He has a mathematical mind and is good at problem solving. Therefore, he likes puzzles and mysteries. His favorite book is about Sherlock Holmes.
- He is good at making reproductive art.
- Christopher understands and relates to animals. He is a humanist and a naturalist. He is able to care for and about animals like Wellington and his pet rat, Toby.
- Christopher is honest to a fault, because he cannot conceive of creating complex illusions or having conditional motives. For Christopher, promises are sacred. He is unable to lie.
- Christopher knows instinctively how to calm himself in stressful situations by reciting math problems and formulas. He is also capable of freeing his mind through detachment, a skill which allows his rational thinking process to take over.
- He has definite goals and dreams. He wants to become an astronaut, obtain a university education, become a professor, and marry.

notes

CANNOT DO:

- Christopher cannot relate well to people, including those he knows. He especially distrusts strangers.
- Christopher does not understand metaphors or non-concrete symbols even when they may represent concrete subjects.
- He has no emotional perspective and relies on his observational skills for most of his information. He cannot read body language because it requires metaphorical interpretation.
- Christopher has no sense of humor. He does not understand idioms or irony and has difficulty with nuances and degrees of definition.
- Christopher is not spiritual by nature, because he cannot logically prove concepts like God and heaven.
- He cannot multi-task and he does not like to know or learn new things, but is willing to accept new things if they are an extension of things he already knows.
- He does not like to be touched; therefore his range of giving and receiving affection is highly limited.

Christopher finds Wellington, the neighbor's dog, dead – killed with a garden tool. His empathy for animals leads him to wonder who would do such a dastardly deed. For Christopher, the existence of this question is a mystery. A mystery is, in turn, a problem waiting to be solved. Since Christopher loves to solve problems, he decides to take on this task.

- Although Christopher would never consider problem solving to be a method of personal growth, that is what happens. Christopher's logical problem-solving process leads him in directions he doesn't anticipate, nor feels comfortable with. As his choices become more limited and urgent, he must weigh one difficult choice against another. As he does this, Christopher bravely extends the boundaries of his knowledge and experience and, in this way, he matures.

- Christopher's story is the teenage version of the children's tale "**The Little Engine That Could,**" whose mantra *"I think I can"* becomes Christopher's tale. With his successes, Christopher realizes he can do anything he sets his mind on. He gains courage and insight. And we are right beside him on the track cheering him along.

> *And I thought, 'I can do this,' because I was doing really well and I was in London and I would find my mother.* (p.172)

> *And I know I can do this because I went to London on my own, and because I solved the mystery of WHO KILLED WELLINGTON? and I found my mother and I was brave and I wrote a book and that means I can do anything.* (p.221)

Christopher's Parents   *Ed and Judy*

- Haddon is very successful at portraying the stress and anguish of parents who are unprepared and ill equipped to deal with a child like Christopher. Even more extraordinary is that we see their difficulties through Christopher's eyes.

- Christopher lives with his father because he believes that his mother has died. His father has made up this story because he did not want to risk Christopher's reaction. He believed that Christopher would not have been able to understand the complicated sexual and emotional relationships that his mother and father had with the respective Mr. and Mrs. Shears. His mother had run off with Roger Shears, and for a short time, his father had a revengeful relationship with Mrs. Shears. As readers, we discover this when Christopher does.

> *Then he said, 'I didn't know what to say ... I was in such a mess ... She left a note and ... Then she rang and ... I said she was in hospital because ... because I didn't know how to explain. It was so difficult ... but once I'd said that ... I couldn't change it. Do you understand ... Christopher ...? ... It just got out of control and I wish ...* (p.114)

- When Judy, Christopher's mom, is told that all of her letters to Christopher had been hidden from him, she makes a *"loud wailing noise like an animal on a nature program on television."* (p.193) Her behavior in this nerve-racking situation is similar to Christopher's in any number of the situations that he finds stressful. This comparison is all the more powerful because Christopher has identified this response through the boundaries of his own experience and understanding:

> *... there was sweat running down my face from under my hair and I was moaning, not groaning, but different, like a dog when it has hurt its paw, and I heard the sound but I didn't realize it was me at first.* (p.176)

- Over the years, Christopher's parents have worked out their own approaches to Christopher using, for example, the hand-fan to signify affection and hugs. Despite their limitations, there is no denying the love that each of his parents has for Christopher.

> *Father ... held up his right hand and spread his fingers out in a fan. I held up my left hand and spread my fingers out in a fan and we made our fingers and thumbs touch each other. We do this because sometimes Father wants to give me a hug, but I do not like hugging people so we do this instead, and it means that he loves me.* (p.16)

- It is clear from Christopher's observation that his parents have had a troubled relationship, but Christopher himself does not conclude that their difficulties have had anything to do with him. As readers, we are able to consider the impact of having to deal with a child such as Christopher, or a child with any physical, mental or emotional difficulty.

Consider this point in your discussion.

Mr. and Mrs. Shears

- Roger and Eileen are neighbors to the Boones. Mr. Shears and Christopher's mother begin an affair and leave their respective spouses. Christopher's father and Mrs. Shears comfort each other in a sexual relationship. This situation does not work, and in a fit of frustration and anger over his wife's adulterous relationship, Christopher's father first lies to Christopher about his mother, and later kills Wellington, the Shears' dog, in reaction to hurtful comments made to him by Mrs. Shears.

- Christopher's father is left alone to care for Christopher. Even as a couple, Christopher's parents found it difficult to manage. As single parents, Christopher's father, and later his mother, have an even more stressful time.

- When Christopher learns both truths, he is forced to make a tough decision – with whom should he live? Christopher takes us through the process of his decision-making and his actions. His fear of his father leads him to find his mother and both parents come slowly back into Christopher's life. His mother moves back to rented rooms in their town, Swindon, and his father remains in the family home.

notes

Mrs. Alexander and Siobhan

- Both Mrs. Alexander and Siobhan have a sympathetic and respectful attitude to Christopher. They each make Christopher feel comfortable and, as a result, they each help him to grow and develop skills beyond his familiar boundaries.

- When Christopher first meets his neighbor, Mrs. Alexander, in the course of his investigation, she is a stranger to him. His fear of strangers is overridden by the fact that he is doing important detective work, and by the fact that she has a pet dog.

- In their conversation, Christopher realizes that Mrs. Alexander is doing *"what is called chatting, where people say things to each other which aren't questions and answers and aren't connected."* (p.40) Even though this makes Christopher feel uncomfortable, he responds to her interest in him as a person. He also concludes that because she owns a dog, she therefore must like dogs. Christopher's logical extension of this thought is that Mrs. Alexander must then be a good person to talk to.

- Siobhan is a trained professional who deals intuitively with Christopher on his own level. When Christopher is confronted with mixed messages from other people, for example, the use of metaphor, or other behavior that bends or breaks the rules, he doesn't know what to do or how to react. This can cause him distress and causes others to respond to him in frustration or in anger. At times like this, it is Siobhan who understands Christopher and streamlines his comprehension by reducing instructions to a basic, logical and sequential series of actions:

    > *Siobhan understands. When she tells me not to do something she tells me exactly what it is that I am not allowed to do. And I like this.* (p.29)

- It is Siobhan who encourages Christopher to write his novel, which in effect is a journal. This has two purposes:

  - First, it helps Christopher organize and record his thoughts. It gives Christopher many opportunities to review and reflect on his thoughts, actions and reactions. Because it is structured as a mystery story, Christopher not only works on solving the problem of a murdered dog, but he can also work on resolving ideas that he might otherwise not understand – for example, how to deal with a mother who suddenly reappears in his life.

  - Secondly, the novel/journal becomes the vehicle by which the reader learns to understand and appreciate Christopher.

notes

FOCUS POINTS
AND THEMES

Power of Storytelling

Counterexample

Paradox

The Truth about Lies

Safety

Stress

Courage

Trust

FOCUS POINTS AND THEMES

Because of his specific personal experience with autistic individuals and his general interest in the subject of disabilities, Mark Haddon presents this novel with a single goal: to illustrate and normalize the essence of autism and Asperger's syndrome.

In Christopher, we have a person whose behavior is seen by others as decidedly odd. By allowing us to hear from Christopher himself, we are forced to confront our personal reactions to him and to evaluate where his unusual behavior stands juxtaposed to our own "odd" behavior.

Haddon uses the following focus points and themes as a place to start our deliberation of this significant human condition.

The Power of Storytelling

... the framework of the story juxtaposed with the framework of the autistic condition

- Stories of all kinds help young children to organize their world and to learn about good and evil, about courage and bravery, about making difficult decisions and about interpreting their outcomes.

- The idea of storytelling and writing centers around the power of imagination, yet Christopher's own powers of imagination are severely limited. However, he is able to expand on and adapt what he already knows by using the language of logic in place of imagination and metaphor. He sees and learns new things through the discovery aspect of the mystery story, a literary style that Christopher likes very much.

- Christopher is the author and the narrator of his own story, a technique that Haddon chooses to use instead of relying on a non-fictional format to explain the mysteries of autistic behavior. **(see Suggested Beginnings, p.7)** According to Haddon, this novel is *"a book about books, about what you can do with words and what it means to communicate with someone in a book."* **(Welch)**

- There are two reasons for Christopher's decision to write his own novel:

  - He likes mysteries primarily because they are puzzles, which he likes to solve, and Christopher wants specifically to solve the puzzle of Wellington's death. He reads the Sherlock Holmes stories and because they are written in novel form, he decides to do the same.

  - On project day, his teacher, Siobhan, suggests that he write about finding Wellington and his experience at the police station.

- While Christopher does not like the idea of *"proper novels,"* (p.19) he does like books. For Christopher, the difference is as follows: novels are fictional, therefore they are about things that are made up and that happen only in the writer's imagination. This idea would normally tend to make Christopher afraid because he would consider a novel to be a lie. Christopher hates lies.

- Although he does consider the irony of this literary conflict, Christopher makes the decision to solve Wellington's murder by recording both his experiences and his investigation as a murder mystery novel.

- As the narrator of his own story, Christopher paints the truth as he sees it. True to his psychological framework, Christopher uses only similes, which are words portraying ideas that he can readily understand. He leaves the larger metaphors to us.

- There would normally be no other way to intimately get to know someone like Christopher, because he would never give anyone the chance. But because this novel is so well constructed, the reader can enter Christopher's mind and thoughts more easily and naturally. Such is the power of a story.

Counterexample

- Christopher is different from other children and attends a school for children with special needs. Society has defined and identified the behavioral characteristics that lead to his placement in this special environment. Although Haddon, himself, never labels Christopher, it is understood that Christopher suffers from Asperger's Syndrome.
  (see Last Thoughts, p.58)

- Christopher challenges the definition of "special needs," although he does not challenge his placement in such a school. There is a measure of safety for Christopher to be surrounded by trained professionals who can help him develop his skills. They teach him to function in the outer world where he faces reactions such as the policeman's *"you are a bloody handful, you are, Jeez"* (p.160) or by the man who tried to save Christopher from being hit by the subway train: *"Mad as a fucking hatter. Jesus."* (p.184)

- Christopher, the character and the narrator, is Haddon's proof that there is no simple, straightforward definition for autism or Asperger's. (see Key to the Novel, p.11) Haddon takes society's commonly shared experiences and feelings about Christopher's condition and converts them into counterexamples. For example, Christopher exhibits autistic behaviors and is considered to be autistic. Other people who exhibit many of these same behaviors are not labeled autistic. Thus the converse of the statement about autism can be false. (see Triangle, p.52)

Paradox

The idea of paradox is an extension of the idea of counterexamples.

Christopher's story, and indeed Christopher himself, is filled with paradox – ideas that seem illogical or contradictory but that actually illustrate certain truths.

- Christopher is quick to tell us he has no sense of humor, but there is much humor in his telling of the story.

- As the narrator, Christopher accomplishes what many writers dream of achieving – to tell a story without complication and to leave the reactions and conclusions entirely up to the reader.

- Christopher has an emotional range of zero. He cannot cry, and although he can feel either sad or happy, there are no nuances in between. Yet, in the novel, there is an emotional component to everything that Christopher does and discovers – for example, the murder of the dog, the discovery of his mother's disappearance and reappearance, his distress over the knowledge that he may not be able to take his math exam, his pride at having surmounted the many obstacles on his way to London.

- Christopher's voice is the narrative voice of the novel. But a real Christopher would be unable to write a book such as this because he would not be able to place himself into any situation other than his own. He would never be able to enter the thoughts of another person. (see Theory of Mind, p.60) The novel's Christopher is completely true to his own perspective, yet the reader is keenly aware of Christopher's thoughts, reactions and motivation, as well as those of his parents and the many others with whom he comes into contact.

- In a traditional fiction book, the narrator uses metaphors, imagery and symbolism to help define and detail the story. In this way, the narrative can bend and twist into shades of truth, for the purpose of illuminating that truth. Christopher cannot tell a lie. This novel is a made-up story about a character who only knows how to tell the truth.

- While Christopher fears strangers, the reader is made keenly aware of how the strangers really fear someone like Christopher. The reactions Christopher gets from people range from empathetic (Mrs. Alexander) to abusive (the policeman and the man in the subway).

The most obvious paradox is that Christopher, with his unusual and literal view of people and the world, has a deep and philosophical appreciation for life and the living. His poignant perspective contrasts with the often complicated, untruthful, simplistic, and cynical view of the so-called "normal" people around him.

notes

The Truth About Lies

- Christopher cannot tell lies, not because he is a good person as his mother tells him, but because *"A lie is when you say something happened which didn't happen."* (p.19) The danger in talking about things that haven't happened is that it opens the possibilities of talking about dozens or hundreds of things which never happened. Therefore, the lie, within this definition, has no boundaries. Christopher needs boundaries in order to feel safe.

- Christopher cannot differentiate the shades of grey that lie between the blacks and the whites of truth, and therefore Christopher dismisses all lies. Christopher's logic allows for no exceptions or nuances.

- Christopher's thoughts on the nature of lies and truth reveal to us that our own views of a lie depend on a mixture of content, situation, motivation, and relationship.

- Christopher's perspective is usually all or nothing. However, Christopher does develop a sense of lying through omission, which is the basis of something called a white lie.

    A white lie is not a lie at all. It is where you tell the truth but you do not tell all of the truth. (p.48)

- Despite his promise to his father that he won't pursue his investigation, Christopher manages to circumvent his promise by logically working through the possible questions he might ask Mrs. Alexander. Christopher is determined to arrive at a level of truth that ranks higher on his ethical scale than his promise to his father.

- Christopher dislikes Sir Arthur Conan Doyle because Doyle had dabbled in spiritualism, something for which Christopher has no patience and which Christopher believes is not true. Christopher does not believe you can communicate with the dead and he understands that things like photography can be altered to show that

notes

fairies do not really exist. Christopher understands the complex human idea that *" ... sometimes people want to be stupid and they do not want to know the truth."* (p.90)

Safety

- Christopher feels safe only when his life is ordered and repetitive. He likes knowing what to expect and so follows a written schedule of his day. He devises his own sets of rules and expectations and so he classifies his days into Good Days, Bad Days, Super Good or Super Bad Days, Black Days, etc., and he rarely deviates from them.

  > *I don't like it when I put things on my timetable and I have to take them out again, because when I do that it makes me feel sick.* (p.212)

- Christopher has a favorite dream where all the people of the world have disappeared except the *"people who don't look at other people's faces ... all special people like me."* (p.198, 199) The safety factor for Christopher in such a situation would mean that he could do what he liked without having to explain or change in order to accommodate the expectations of others. For Christopher, this would be the ultimate freedom.

- Safety, for Christopher, is knowing what to expect without surprises. He is apprehensive about entering his mother's London flat because he has never been there before. Alternatively, he feels much better about the workings of the train station once he realizes that the information being offered is programmed by a computer.

  > *And then I heard the sound like sword fighting and the roaring of a train coming into the station and I worked out that there was a big computer somewhere and it knew where all the trains were and it sent messages to the black boxes in the little stations to say when the trains were coming, and that made me feel better because everything had an order and a plan.* (p.181)

Stress

- Stress is a common human condition and the things that Christopher finds stressful are not unusual; it is his reaction to that stress and his coping strategies that may be more limiting for him than for the general public. If Christopher were to exhibit only one or two of these distinctive qualities, he could be viewed as eccentric. But he exhibits a great many of these traits, each with an inappropriate intensity.

- When Christopher is under extreme stress, he fails to notice things in his usual detailed way: *"...there were too many things to look at and too many things to hear."* **(p.145)**

- Christopher has difficulty operating outside the boundaries of his organized life. Because his problems make him feel uncomfortable, Christopher does not like putting himself in new situations, and as a result, he has never had to test his levels of courage. Finding the strength to run away from his father becomes for Christopher the ultimate test. The stress in this situation becomes a positive force for change.

Courage

- Christopher doesn't think in terms of courage, but rather in terms of challenge. He believes that there is always an answer available through math. Finding it just takes time.

- For Christopher, the commonplace act of being in a public subway station is *"like standing on a cliff in a really strong wind ... like stepping off the cliff on a tightrope."* **(p.145)** This is a wonderful image for Christopher, because it does not refer to death, but to balance. It is balance that is Christopher's greatest challenge and Christopher needs to use his courage to find this balance.

- He also needs his courage to make decisions, something Christopher is less comfortable with because doing so requires a degree of intuition. He is able to make decisions only when there are two concrete alternatives with which he is familiar. Christopher eventually gains the courage to make decisions based on unknown outcomes, emotions, and facts.

- When he is confronted with a no-choice situation, Christopher slowly learns to see past the chaos and confusion. For example, when he buys his train ticket to London, the ticket is half yellow, and Christopher dislikes yellow. However, Christopher knows that this ticket is his passage, and that it is not in his best interest to avoid it. By pretending he is in a computer game, and by repeating a rhythmic mantra, he is able to minimize the chaotic fear he feels. **(p.154)**

- Deciding between two alternatively bad choices is a mature concept and Christopher begins to make the best of the bad choices he faces. Instead of being frozen and unable to act, Christopher seems motivated by the stress of his possible outcomes. By choosing to go to London to seek out his mother, Christopher finds himself out of his comfort zone and this causes him great fear. But there is a still greater fear in remaining with his father. Christopher replaces a less manageable fear with a more manageable one:

  > *I had to work out what to do.*
  >
  > *And I did this by thinking of all the things I could do and deciding whether they were the right decision or not.*
  >
  > *I decided that I couldn't go home again.*
  >
  > *... the thought of going somewhere on my own was frightening. But then I thought about going home again, or staying where I was, or hiding in the garden every night and Father finding me, and that made me feel even more frightened. And when I thought about that I felt like I was going to be sick again...* **(p.129, 130)**

- One of the best coping skills that Siobhan teaches him is to comfort himself with repetition, and so Christopher counts. He does math problems in his head, or he marches to a rhythm. It is the same coping mechanism that religious people use when they finger a rosary or say a prayer or meditate. It is the same process that Pi uses in Yann Martel's wonderful novel, **Life of Pi**.

> *And then I realized that there was nothing I could do which felt safe. And I made a picture of it in my head ...*
>
> *And then I imagined crossing out all the possibilities which were impossible.* (p.130)

Trust

- For Christopher, the concept of trust is black and white – either it is there or it is not. He trusts only his parents and his teacher, and cannot trust anyone he does not know. He has virtually no contact with anyone else. But, in time, he comes to trust Mrs. Alexander.

- Christopher had trusted his father to deal with him truthfully because he had no reason nor experience to expect otherwise. But Christopher's father has broken his trust with Christopher when he admits to killing the dog. He also confesses to and is remorseful about lying to Christopher about his mother.

- While Christopher's dad expresses his regrets and promises never to do such a thing again, his admission lies in the place where trust is not black and white, but has shades of grey. Christopher is not equipped to deal with shades of grey and so is distraught by his father's lies.

> *I had to get out of the house. Father had murdered Wellington. That meant he could murder me, because I couldn't trust him, even though he had said "Trust*

me," because he had told a lie about a big thing. **(p.122)**

- Eventually, Christopher's father asks Christopher to allow him to rebuild his "honesty" with Christopher. When he buys Christopher a new dog, it is part of a teachable process organized to have a projected outcome – the establishment of new trust. Christopher is learning something new about trust.

Making Decisions

- If we were to devise a formula for making proper decisions, it would include, in combination, the elements of safety, stress, courage, and trust. On the other hand, Christopher, who likes prime numbers, reduces decision making to its prime elements:

  ... in life you have to take lots of decisions and if you don't take decisions you would never do anything because you would spend all your time choosing between things you could do. So it is good to have a reason why you hate some things and you like others ... [when faced with likes and dislikes, you choose only the likes] ... and then it is simple. **(p.85)**

- We might all be better off using Christopher's formula to make our own decisions.

The Power of Teaching

- Christopher's teacher, Siobhan, is a thought-provoking character. She is very supportive of Christopher as a teacher should be, and she has many practical suggestions and skills for Christopher. She is a counterbalance to Christopher's parents.

- Both of Christopher's parents love him unconditionally, but clearly have difficulty dealing full time with his special needs. Without professional experience and specialized knowledge, his parents are at a disadvantage. They cannot manage Christopher and have allowed their own "needs" to get in the way of their care for their son. Christopher needs a competent coach by his side.

- Enter Siobhan, who raises the reader's awareness of the need for a good teacher.

How would Christopher have developed without the expertise and caring of someone like Siobhan? Do others like Christopher have the potential for independent living?

Should more time, money, and effort be spent in developing suitable supportive environments for children like Christopher? How would Christopher have fared with a less sensitive support worker?

Discuss the power and effect of good teaching.

WRITING STYLE AND STRUCTURE

Grammar

Narration

Story Structure

WRITING STYLE AND STRUCTURE

Grammar

- Haddon's written language and sentence structure mimics Christopher's simple subject-verb-object pattern of speech. The construction of simple sentences and paragraphs is a fundamental grammar used both by teachers of the young and by English-as-a-Second-Language teachers. It is basic language and grammar reduced to its prime status, uncomplicated by adjective and adverb phrasing, conjunctive clauses, and sentence reversals. It comes across most clearly in the similes (not metaphors) that Christopher uses.

- Christopher is able to understand similes that use the comparison words, 'like' and 'as', because they juxtapose two familiar and concrete images. He has difficulty with metaphors that compare without the use of help-words and that rely on a more subtle, abstract understanding based outside of normal experience.

Narration

- Haddon's novel is told in the first person by Christopher, a highly functional person with Asperger's Syndrome who, despite defining himself as non-intuitive, is nevertheless able to give us accurate, detailed descriptions and observations from behind the veil of Asperger's.

- Where a third-person-narrative with a strong research base might be considered more intellectually authoritative, Christopher's voice and perspective cannot be dismissed. He legitimately describes his first-hand reactions and detailed explanations to the world around him.

- Christopher's book, a mystery novel, is a metaphor for the mystery surrounding Asperger's. But Christopher, himself, does not like metaphors because he finds their subtlety difficult to understand. He gives an example:

  > In proper novels people say things like, "I am veined with iron, with silver and with streaks of common mud. I cannot contract into the firm fist which those clench who do not depend on stimulus." **(p.4, 5)**

- This passage, which Christopher claims to have found in a library book, is quite perplexing, even for a sophisticated reader. Christopher has made an insightful point.

- The use of this example is quite humorous and is another subtle undertone that Haddon introduces. Christopher has an understated sense of humor of which he is oblivious, which develops as his story continues. Although he claims to not have the ability to tell jokes, he does eventually tell a joke; in fact, he tells three jokes. **(p.143)**

Story Structure

- Christopher has written a novel that parallels a regular novel by using similar literary techniques: a number of linked characters, plot structure, chapter divisions, drama, climax and a satisfactory conclusion.

- Christopher has numbered all his chapters not in sequential chronological order, but by prime numbers. **(see Prime Numbers, p.51)**

- Through Christopher's written narration, Haddon offers up a fiction that is part diary, part memoir, part non-fiction and includes an appendix used, as appendixes are, for in-depth explanation.

SYMBOLS

Prime Numbers

Okapi

Triangle

Tightrope Walker

SYMBOLS

There are four significant symbols used by Christopher to represent himself: a prime number, the okapi, a triangle, and a tightrope walker.

Prime Numbers

- Christopher is a human being like all others, but with a symbolic twist. Christopher is a prime number, a human being stripped of all extraneous and symbolic human characteristics. A prime number is not divisible by any other number; it is unique. This is Christopher, a person who is simple and simply himself.

- Haddon has cleverly used Christopher as a metaphor for himself. He has no overlapping figurative layers, nor does he understand them. To himself, he is very logical; to others, he appears incomprehensible.

- The chapters are sequential, but are numbered with prime numbers (2, 3, 5, 7 etc.) instead of the usual cardinal numbers (1, 2, 3, etc.)

  Prime numbers are what is left when you have taken all the patterns away. I think prime numbers are like life. They are very logical but you could never work out the rules, even if you spent all your time thinking about them. (p.12)

Okapi

- When he considers his recurring dreams, Christopher realizes that there may be other survivors like himself, but he doesn't see them. He refers to them as okapi, a rarely seen and extremely shy African antelope. The okapi has mythical qualities, much like the unicorn.

- This image suits Christopher well because he is also extremely shy, and were it not for his book, he would rarely be seen as a sympathetic and individual personality. He would be viewed as a complex individual – mysterious and limited.

Triangle

- The Pythagorean formula is a consistent theory explaining that a right-angled triangle occurs when a triangle has two of its sides at a right-angle. The sum of the squares of those sides equals the length of hypotenuse, the third side, squared. (see Pythagoras, p.60)

- On his math test, Christopher is asked to prove that not all triangles whose sides fit together as right angles follow this formula. It is possible for a right-angled triangle to have a different formula.

- We are meant to think of Christopher in the following way: although the characteristics of his personality and his behavior fit the clinical definition (formula) of Asperger's, many of these qualities are also evident in the general public. If the triangle represents the mainstream of society, then Christopher also belongs. Christopher is simply the triangle whose sides fit a different formula. **(see Counterexample, p.11, p.33)**

Tightrope Walker

- What defines Christopher is his need for boundaries. While everyone would prefer to have recognizable boundaries, Christopher has a greater need for structural limits, because that is how he feels safe. For most people, it is the crossing of these boundaries that leads to their personal achievements. It may take some risk, frustration and emotional anxiety, but most people will trust and hope that a parachute will be found and the landing will be safe.

- Christopher does not have the comfort of understanding this metaphor. For Christopher, overstepping the boundaries of his world and knowledge is like walking off a cliff onto a tightrope. By adding the image of a tightrope to the image of the cliff, Haddon instantly takes the experience out of the reader's realm and places it in Christopher's. **(see Courage, p.38)** For Christopher, any crossing of familiar lines is fraught with danger. The tightrope represents Christopher's ever-present struggle to retrieve his balance and to stay upright while navigating over a chasm of obstacles.

- Christopher has a dream where he is left alone in the world. **(p.198)** As a single survivor of a deadly virus, Christopher feels safe despite the open and empty space around him. His feeling of safety comes from not having to negotiate with others for the space in his environment. Being alone is what gives him control.

LAST THOUGHTS

LAST THOUGHTS

- Siobhan suggests to Christopher that he use his appendix as the place to lay out the full explanation of his counterexample formula. She tells him that

  > ... *people wouldn't want to read the answers to a maths question in a book [and that he should] put the answer in an Appendix, which is an extra chapter at the end of a book which people can read if they want to.* (p.214)

- Haddon takes this idea to heart and therefore does not include lengthy explanations about autism, Asperger's syndrome, or other technical information. In keeping with this role model, this guide's section called **LAST THOUGHTS** is a useful place to define the technical terms that Haddon leaves out.

Autism

Autism is classified as a pervasive developmental disorder and has several manifestations, one of which is Asperger's syndrome. Other disorders can border on mental retardation, e.g. Rett's Syndrome or Childhood Disintegrative Disorder.

The characteristics that define autism are severe and include the following:

- significant difficulties with social interactions – does not pay attention to other people; does not play with other children; does not reciprocate

- significant difficulties in verbal and nonverbal communication – grabs what is wanted; copies or parrots words (echolalia); if the child has words, the child may not use them to converse with others

- significant difficulties in the development of play skills – uses only parts of toys; lines up or stacks objects; no imaginative play

- highly restricted, repetitive and stereotyped patterns of behavior and interests – may talk continuously about one topic or repeat the same questions; may spin and stare at objects; may flap fingers or pieces of string; or hit himself

- highly resistant to even slight changes in routines

Asperger's Syndrome

Sometimes referred to as Asperger's Disorder, Asperger's Syndrome is a neurobiological disorder, which describes a pattern of unusual behavior in young boys, and occasionally in girls, who otherwise display normal intelligence and language development. Their unusual behavior characteristics include a lack of social and communication skills. It is named for Hans

Asperger, a doctor from Vienna, who first published a paper on the subject in 1944.

The characteristics of this disorder can range from mild to severe. The features of this syndrome include the following:

- difficulty with transition or change

- obsessive routines, which concentrate on maintaining a "sameness"

- a normal or exceptional IQ which may include a talent or strong interest in a subject

- difficulty reading body language and other nonverbal clues

- highly sensitive to sound, taste, smell and sight – leading to strong food and other aversions or preferences

- odd and unusual perception of the surrounding environment

- easily bullied; socially awkward

- children identified as having Asperger's Syndrome are often initially and wrongly diagnosed with ADD (Attention Deficit Disorder) or ADHD (Attention Deficit Hyper-activity Disorder).

- children with Asperger's Disorder can learn social skills by rote

Christopher himself lists all the characteristics of his own behavioral situation on pages 46 and 47 of the novel.

Theory of Mind

- The term "theory of mind" is from a 1978 article called *"Does the Chimpanzee have a Theory of Mind?"* and was published in the journal, **Behavioral and Brain Sciences 4:515-526,** by D. Premack and G. Woodruff. This term explains that according to normal psychological development, all people have the ability to consciously know and understand the fact that everyone else also knows things and thinks of ideas. The essence of this knowledge is that someone else's thoughts and ideas may be different from one's own. This awareness is a crucial psychological developmental step in children.

- It is this developmental awareness that is missing in autistic or Asperger's individuals. These people tend to develop the theory of mind late, or not at all. Psychological research in this area has shown that learned behaviors, like language, can increase this awareness to a certain extent. This is Christopher's situation.

- Because of his considerable language and math skills, he is aware that others think differently from himself, but he is unable to process or recognize the motivational component behind their thoughts. He simply does not understand them.

Pythagoras

- Pythagoras of Samos (540-500 B.C.) was a Greek philosopher who taught religion and ethics in the area known today as Italy. Over time, Pythagoras has come to represent great learning and wisdom.

- Like Christopher, Pythagoras loved mysteries and he established a number of theories aimed at solving the unknown or ambiguous elements of human thought. His theories use number symbolism beyond the level of counting and measuring.

notes

- In pursuing numbers as a basis for his theory, Pythagoras aimed to prove the existence of harmony in the world. He established geometry and mathematics as a method of proving that the world has a balanced and organized structure that can be easily understood through numbers.

- One of his theories, the Pythagorean theorem, states that the square of the hypotenuse of a right-angled triangle is equal to the sum of the squares of the other two sides. This is true, but although all right-angled triangles will conform to that formula, some right-angled triangles can be made up of different measurements. (see Triangle, p.52)

- It is this counterexample that Christopher seeks to apply to himself. Just as all right-angled triangles do not fit the usual formula, so too, Christopher does not exactly fit the common perception and definition of people with autism/Asperger's. (see Counterexample, p.11, p.33; see Triangle, p.52)

What We Learn from Christopher

- We learn not to prejudge Christopher and others like him.

  > ... because nothing can travel faster than the speed of light, this means that we can only know about a fraction of the things that go on in the universe ... [or in someone's mind] (p.157)

- Christopher explains that most people are not sufficiently observant, a fact that may explain the existence of snap judgments and preconceived notions.

  > ... most people are almost blind and they don't see most things and there is lots of spare capacity in their heads and it is filled with things which aren't connected and are silly ... (p.144)

- Christopher shows that in order to be a thoughtful human being, one must learn to think beyond oneself, a concept which neither of Christopher's parents seem able to fully do. Yet, Christopher knows intuitively that he cannot take Toby to London because Toby will not get the care he needs. Christopher will have too much else to think about.

- Through Christopher's story, we learn that people can grow despite their handicaps. All they need is the right amount of positive stress, a few positive coping skills, and if possible, the right teacher.

- We watch Christopher as he presents truth both in its variations and its absolute form. To do this, Christopher uses the analogy of constellations – the stars are very real and true; but the pictorial representations that people have created in order to put the vastness of the universe into a manageable perspective are untrue.

  > People say that Orion is call Orion because Orion was a hunter and the constellation looks like a hunter with a club and a bow and arrow …
  >
  > But this is really silly because it is just stars, and you could join up the dots in any way you wanted, and you could make it look like a lady with an umbrella who is waving …
  >
  > … Orion is not a hunter or a coffeemaker or a dinosaur. It is just Betelgeuse and Bellatrix and Alnilam and Rigel and 17 other stars I don't know the names of. And they are nuclear explosions billions of miles away.
  >
  > And that is the truth. (p.125-126)

- We learn from Christopher that ultimately most things are solvable if we take the time to puzzle them out. Christopher compares the complications of the human mind to the detailed complex workings of a computer. This analogy is clear, precise, and reassuring.

... when I was little I didn't understand about other people having minds. And Julie said to Mother and Father that I would always find this very difficult. But I don't find this difficult now. Because I decided that it was a kind of puzzle, and if something is a puzzle there is always a way of solving it.

It's like computers ...

... the mind is just a complicated machine. **(p.116)**

- Christopher is sufficiently aware of human differences to recognize that the difference between the pictures in his head and the pictures in the heads of others is similar to the difference between real concrete happenings and imaginary or speculative happenings. He reminds us to be sensitive to people like his grandmother, who likely suffered from dementia.

  ... Grandmother has pictures in her head, too, but her pictures are all confused, like someone has muddled the film up and she can't tell what happened in what order ... **(p.79)**

- The psychological definition of autism states that autistic people have little expression of emotion. Christopher shows us that this is untrue, that there is another way to view and understand emotionality.

  ... people think they're not computers because they have feelings and computers don't have feelings. But feelings are just having a picture on the screen in your head of what is going to happen tomorrow or next year, or what might have happened instead of what did happen, and if it is a happy picture they smile and if it is a sad picture they cry. **(p.119)**

Haddon's Success

- Mark Haddon has created a story that crosses all age boundaries: the story of a powerless person who prevails in spite of his disabilities or limitations.

- Haddon has fused all his literary, mathematical, experiential, and intuitive skills into the structure of this novel. At the same time, he has reduced everything to its basic elements supported by strong examples shown through Christopher. While Christopher uses the straightforward simile to illustrate an idea, Haddon uses Christopher together with his explanations as a larger metaphor. This gives the book its significance and its sophistication. Like children's literature and fairytales, **the curious incident of the dog in the nighttime** can be read and understood on many levels.

- Christopher's first-person narrative does not allow the reader to distance himself or herself from Christopher's character. There is no safety zone created by a third person narrative or by a factual discussion of autism or Asperger's Syndrome. The reader must deal with this special needs person head-on.

- Haddon presents the revealing, but not sensational, fact that people like Christopher do not differ from others in major ways. Christopher is absolutely human, like the rest of us, in his hopes, dreams, wishes, fears, likes, and dislikes. His coping mechanisms are similar to our own. There are small differences in the intensity of his reactions and in the ease of his interpersonal relationships. But clearly, the fact remains, that there are many people in society who display many of Christopher's characteristics and who are not labeled autistic.

- After the reading of this novel, both the adolescent and adult reader will have a greater understanding of what a child like Christopher and his parents must go through in their daily lives. Understanding

notes

breeds acceptance; acceptance breeds comfort. Haddon has provided some comfort to parents and children alike who are affected by autism and by Asperger's syndrome. As Christopher believes, a little knowledge goes a long way.

Christopher's Conclusion

- Christopher learns that sometimes a person's life goals must be realigned and redefined. At the beginning of the novel, Christopher felt he would make a good astronaut.

    > *... to be a good astronaut you have to be intelligent and I'm intelligent. You also have to understand how machines work and I'm good at understanding how machines work. You also have to be someone who would like being on their own in a tiny spacecraft ... and not panic or get claustrophobia or homesick or insane. And I like really little spaces, so long as there is no one else in them with me.* **(p.50)**

- With his ability to think logically, Christopher realizes that his dream of becoming an astronaut will never happen because it means being away from home. Although his courage has taken him from Swindon to London, it will never be big enough to take him to outer space. The understanding that his dream is just that, a dream, is another example of Christopher's developmental growth. In the end, Christopher is satisfied to take further A-level tests, to go to university in another town, to get his First Class Honors degree and to become a scientist.

    > *And I know I can do this because I went to London on my own, and because I solved the mystery of* **Who Killed Wellington?** *and I found my mother and I was brave and I wrote a book and that means I can do anything.* **(p.221)**

Add any other conclusions or insights that you feel Christopher has to offer.

FROM THE NOVEL

Quotes

FROM THE NOVEL ...

Memorable Quotes from the text of the curious incident of the dog in the night-time

PAGE 1. It was 7 minutes after midnight. The dog was lying on the grass in the middle of the lawn in front of Mrs. Shears's house. Its eyes were closed. It looked as if it was running on its side, the way dogs run when they think they are chasing a cat in a dream. But the dog was not running or asleep. The dog was dead.

PAGE 4, 5. This is a murder mystery novel. Siobhan said that I should write something I would want to read myself. Mostly I read books about science and maths. I do not like proper novels. Siobhan said that the book should begin with something to grab people's attention. That is why I started with the dog. I also started with the dog because it happened to me and I find it hard to imagine things which did not happen to me.

PAGE 7. [The policeman] was asking too many questions and he was asking them too quickly. They were stacking up in my head like loaves in the factory where Uncle Terry works. The factory is a bakery and he operates the slicing machines. And sometimes a slicer is not working fast enough but the bread keeps coming and there is a blockage. I sometimes think of my mind as a machine, but not always as a bread-slicing machine. It makes it easier to explain to other people what is going on inside it.

PAGE 14. It was nice in the police cell. It was almost a perfect cube, 2 meters long by 2 meters wide by 2 meters high. It contained approximately 8 cubic meters of air. It had a small window with bars and ... on the opposite side, a metal door with a long, thin hatch near the floor for sliding trays of food into the cell and a sliding hatch higher up so that policemen could look in and check that prisoners hadn't escaped or committed suicide ...

I wondered how I would escape if I was in a story.

PAGE 15. The word metaphor means carrying something from one place to another ... and it is when you describe something by using a word for something that it isn't. This means that the word metaphor is a metaphor. I think it should be called a lie because a pig is not like a day and people do not have skeletons in their cupboards ... [a metaphor] makes you forget what the person was talking about.

PAGE 21. At 2:07 a.m. I decided that I wanted a drink ... so I went downstairs to the kitchen. Father was sitting on the sofa watching snooker on the television and drinking scotch. There were tears coming out of his eyes. I asked, "Are you sad about Wellington?" He looked at me for a long time and sucked air in through his nose. Then he said, "Yes, Christopher, you could say that. You could very well say that." I decided to leave him alone because when I am sad I want to be left alone ...

PAGE 22, 23. Mother died 2 years ago ... Father said, "I'm afraid you won't be seeing your mother for a while." He didn't look at me when he said this. He kept on looking through the window. Usually people look at you when they're talking to you. I know that they're working out what I'm thinking, but I can't tell what they're thinking. It is like being in a room with a one-way mirror in a spy film. But this was nice, having Father speak to me but not look at me ... "Your mother has had to go into hospital ... She has ... a problem with her heart."

PAGE 28. I decided that I was going to find out who killed Wellington even though Father had told me to stay out of other people's business. This is because I do not always do what I am told. And this is because when people tell you what to do it is usually confusing and does not make sense.

PAGE 33. What actually happens when you die is that your brain stops working and your body rots, like Rabbit did when he died and we buried him in the earth at the bottom of the garden. And all his molecules were broken down into other molecules and they went into the earth and were eaten by worms and went into the plants and if we go and dig in the same place in 10 years there will be nothing except his skeleton left. And in 1,000 years even his skeleton will be gone. But that is all right because he is a part of the flowers and the apple tree and the hawthorn bush now.

notes

PAGE 42. ... Mr. Shears was my Prime Suspect. Mr. Shears used to be married to Mrs. Shears and they lived together until two years ago. Then Mr. Shears left and didn't come back. This was why Mrs. Shears came over and did lots of cooking for us after Mother died, because she didn't have to cook for Mr. Shears anymore and she didn't have to stay at home and be his wife. And also Father said that she needed company and didn't want to be on her own.

PAGE 45. I used to think that Mother and Father might get divorced. That was because they had lots of arguments and sometimes they hated each other. This was because of the stress of looking after someone who has Behavioral Problems like I have.

PAGE 49. Father said, "I told you to keep your nose out of other people's business."... Father banged the table with his fist really hard so that the plates and his knife and fork jumped around and my ham jumped sideways so that it touched the broccoli, so I couldn't eat the ham or the broccoli anymore.

PAGE 56. And then I did some reasoning. I reasoned that Father had only made me do a promise about five things ...... And asking about Mr. Shears wasn't any of these things. And if you are a detective you have to Take Risks, and this was a Super Good Day, which meant it was a good day for Taking Risks, so I said [to Mrs. Alexander], "Do you know Mr. Shears?" which was like chatting.

PAGE 69. ... I listened to the sounds in the garden and I could hear a bird singing and I could hear traffic noise which was like the surf on a beach and I could hear someone playing music somewhere and children shouting. And in between these noises, I listened very carefully and stood completely still, I could hear a tiny whining noise inside my ears and the air going in and out of my nose.

PAGE 71, 73. I like The Hound of the Baskervilles because it is a detective story, which means that there are clues and Red Herrings ...I also like The Hound of the Baskervilles because I like Sherlock Holmes and I think that if I were a proper detective he is the kind of detective I would be. He is very intelligent and he solves the mystery and he says 'The world is full of obvious things which nobody by any chance ever observes.' But he notices them, like I do.

PAGE 75. [Siobhan reads Christopher's discovery about the relationship between his mother and Mr. Shears] ... sometimes we get sad about things and we don't like to tell other people ... We like to keep it a secret. Or sometimes we are sad but we don't really know we are sad ... If you do start to feel sad about this, I want you to know that you can come and talk to me about it ... And if you don't feel sad but you just want to talk to me ... that would be OK, too ... And I replied, "But I don't feel sad about it. Because Mother is dead. And because Mr. Shears isn't around anymore. So I would be feeling sad about something that isn't real and doesn't exist. And that would be stupid."

PAGE 82. Father had never grabbed hold of me like that before. Mother had hit me sometimes because she was a very hot-tempered person, which means that she got angry more quickly than other people and she shouted more often. But Father was a more levelheaded person, which means he didn't get angry as quickly and he didn't shout as often. So I was very surprised when he grabbed me.... So I hit him, like I hit the policeman ...

PAGE 91. I wanted to get my book back because I liked writing it. I liked having a project to do and I liked it especially if it was a difficult project like a book. Also I still didn't know who had killed Wellington and my book was where I had kept all the clues that I had discovered and I did not want them to be thrown away.

PAGE 98. ... I was really confused because mother ... had never lived in London ... And Mother had never written a letter to me before ... the letter was posted on 16 October 1997, which was 18 months after Mother had died.

PAGE 112. ... I stopped reading the letter because I felt sick ... the room was swinging from side to side, as if it was at the top of a really tall building and the building was swinging backward and forward in a strong wind (this is a simile ...) But I knew that the room couldn't be swinging backward and forward, so it must have been something which was happening inside my head.

PAGE 120. [Father said] "Look, maybe I shouldn't say this, but ... I want you to know that you can trust me. And ... OK, maybe I don't tell the truth all the time. God knows, I try, Christopher, God knows I do, but ... Life is difficult, you know. It's bloody hard telling th truth all the time. Sometimes it's impossible ... but ... You have to know that I am going to tell you the truth from now on. About everything. Because ... if you don't tell the truth now, then later on ... later on it hurts even more. So ...

PAGE 131, 132. And then I thought how I could never be an astronaut because being an astronaut meant being hundreds of thousands of miles away from home, and my home was in London now ... and thinking about this made me hurt ... But this hurt was inside my head. And it made me sad to think that I could never become an astronaut.

PAGE 137. ... I knew that if I curled up on the ground and did groaning, then Father would come out of the school and ... take me home. So I took lots of deep breaths like Siobhan says I have to do ... I concentrated very hard on the numbers and did their cubes as I said them. And that made the hurt less painful.

PAGE 164, 165. People believe in God because the world is very complicated and they think it is very unlikely that anything as complicated as a flying squirrel or the human eye or a brain could happen by chance ... And people who believe in God think God has put human beings on the earth because they think human beings are the best animal, but human beings are just an animal and they will evolve into another animal ... Or human beings will all catch a disease and die out or they will make too much pollution and kill themselves, and then there will only be insects in the world and they will be the best animal.

PAGE 173. And I did detecting by watching and I saw that people were putting tickets into gray gates and walking through ... And I watched 47 people do this and I memorized what to do ... And someone said, "Get a move on," and I made the noise like a dog barking and I walked forward ...

PAGE 186. And when the train stopped at Willesden Junction and the doors opened automatically I walked out of the train. And then the doors closed and the train went away. And everyone who got off the train walked up a staircase and over a bridge except me ...... I didn't want to talk to [anyone] because I was tired and hungry and I had already talked to lots of strangers, which is dangerous, and the more you do something dangerous the more likely it is that something bad happens. But I didn't know how to get to 451c Chapter Road, London NW2 5NG, so I had to ask somebody.

PAGE 191. And Mother put her arms around me and said, "Christopher, Christopher, Christopher." And I pushed her away because she was grabbing me and I didn't like it, and I pushed really hard and I fell over ...And Mother said, "I'm so sorry, Christopher. I forgot."

notes

ACKNOWLEDGEMENTS